THE HAUNTING OF
M.E.

Brenda L. Murray

INDELIBLE CREATIVE

Cataloguing in Publication information is available from Library and Archives Canada.

Indelible Creative
Pioneer Park Box 20105,
Kitchener, Ontario
N2P2B4
www.indeliblecreative.ca

ISBN 978-0-9735749-4-4

www.facebook.com/TheHauntingOfME

Dedicated to my wonderful family, Dan, Peter, Kaitlin and Danielle Murray.

Table of Contents

Chapter 1

I'm not going to scream, I told myself although panic shot through my body like a jolt of lightning.

My heart pounded. My throat tightened. I peered intensely in every direction but there was no sign of the Comfort Station and no sign of my tent.

It's so dark.

Without thinking, I began stumbling through the woods, my arms outstretched, my eyes wide. I stopped and stared but could see nothing.

I'm not going to scream. I'm not going to scream.

I began running in another direction. Branches scraped my face and tugged at my flannel pyjama bottoms. I pushed them aside. My breath came in gasps.

How did I get myself in this situation?

It started with mosquitoes in the tent; relentless, droning, loud, then quiet, then loud again, as if someone was playing with the volume control. *Stupid mosquitoes,* I thought. *They're really bugging me.*

My hands groped the gritty tent floor for my iPod.

If I listen to some music, it'll take my mind off the mosquitoes.

I felt around the edges of the tent. Nothing.

This is stupid. I need a flashlight.

I wiggled out of the tangled sleeping bag. I felt sweaty and frustrated. I couldn't wait for the weekend to be over. I remade my bed and straightened out my stuff but my iPod didn't turn up. No sign of a flashlight either. I felt the tent floor again and found a bottle of mosquito repellent.

I gave myself a good spritz.

Great, now I smell like a lemon meringue pie.

Scrambling through the woods a lingering waft of citron hit my nose. I pushed aside a branch wet with dew. Random thoughts bounced around my mind. I remembered hearing Dave, my new step-father, snoring like a jack hammer through the thin wall of our tent.

He should get that fixed, I remembered thinking at the time.

Dave, "Mr. Outdoorsy", made the worst campfire chili I'd ever tasted. It was mushy, brown and tasteless.

Why did my mother have to fall in love with a camper?

Then mom's big genuine smile flashed across my mind—duh—dumb question.

At least he married Mom and he's sticking around. Not like my real dad who just disappeared.

I remembered sitting behind Dave on the drive up to Algonquin Park. "Did you know that bug spray will remove tree sap?" he was saying over his shoulder.

"Fascinating, Dave," I said sarcastically.

"Mary Elizabeth", mom said quietly. She saw me roll my eyes and gave me a warning look.

"Always keep a clean campsite," Dave went on. "Burn all food scraps and even the dishwater goes into the fire so you don't attract wild animals."

But I was only half listening. I was trapped in the back seat of our station wagon next to a pile of khaki camping junk that filled the entire back end of the car. Camping advice was the last thing on my mind.

Where did I put my iPod? I wondered, glancing around the car.

"Wolves—now they're the worst," Dave said. "They hunt in packs. But generally, wild animals will stay away if you have a fire burning. Need a pee-break, M.E.?" he asked as he pulled into the Lake of Two Rivers General Store.

Without answering I jumped out of the car, slammed the door behind me and headed straight into the building.

I look terrible, I thought glancing in the bathroom mirror.

I was the first back at the car. It gave me the chance to dig through the camping equipment.

Tent pegs, pots, rubber boots, pack of batteries, food box, flashlight, air mattress pump thingy...ah-ha! I found my iPod.

Now I won't have to listen to any more of Dave's boring outdoor survival tips.

Hours later in the tent, there I was once again searching for that dumb iPod when I realized that I really needed to go to the bathroom but, of course, couldn't find a flashlight either.

I thought about waking up my mom so I could borrow hers but I hadn't spoken to her since our big blow out at the campfire. I knew I was wrong but I wasn't about to wake up my mom to apologize just so I could borrow her flashlight.

Instead, I pulled on my hoodie, unzipped the tent and peered into the blackness in the direction of the park Comfort Station.

Then I spotted a glow between the trees.

That must be the Comfort Station, I thought and headed in that direction.

In the clearing of our campsite, I could only see a few feet in front of me by the light of the moon. The ground was fairly level and strewn with pine needles but when I passed between some trees I tripped on a root. After that, I walked with my arms held out in front of me.

As I got closer to the glow, I could see that it was definitely not the Comfort Station. The light was moving. It was a cloud of many tiny twinkling lights hovering between the trees.

Fireflies!

If I'd had a glass jar I would have tried to capture some. I remembered the "Lightning Bug" presentation that someone at school made last year. The light they produced had something to do with a chemical reaction that occurs in specialized light-emitting organs on their abdomens; but for me, they were magical. They reminded me of pictures of glowing fairies in the fairy tale books my mom used to read to me.

When I was little, the Tooth Fairy used to leave a loonie under my pillow and a tiny note written in a spindly, miniscule script. The Tooth Fairy's note was always very polite and formal. It would talk about what she did with the teeth and it always included a map of our backyard and directions for a scavenger hunt. One of the notes said that fireflies kept the Tooth Fairy's home lit up at night.

I loved those notes and saved them in a shoebox I kept under my bed along with the loonies and some baby pictures. Fireflies were the only kind of insect I've ever really been able to tolerate. Surrounded by them, I tried to catch one in my hand but each time I reached for one its light went out and it disappeared. I tried a few more times to catch one but it was no good.

Gradually I realized that the cloud of fireflies was thinning out. Soon, only a handful flashed their little lights.

I looked back in the direction I had come. It was inky black and unfamiliar. Without realizing it, I'd followed the cloud deeper into the woods.

No! No, no, no, no, no!

I stood in complete darkness with no tent and no Comfort Station in sight. I had no idea from which direction I had come. I was utterly and profoundly lost.

Chapter 2

I'm not going to scream. I'm not going to scream.

I looked around with wide eyes but could see nothing. Then I tried squinting. That wasn't any better.

I'm not like those drama queen girls at school who are always screaming and drawing attention to themselves. They're so lame.

My heart was racing but I resolved to be logical.

No way am I gonna start screaming, I kept telling myself.

I tried to think clearly and not get emotional.

Just when I thought I couldn't hold in the scream any longer, I heard a sound--voices.

Straining, I heard voices but not words, suffixes and prefixes, clips of disjointed phrases, and laughter. The words floated in the air faintly sparking then disappearing like the fireflies. I listened hard but couldn't decide from which direction the voices were coming. I stumbled forward but the words got fainter then vanished altogether.

There was something else, something closer.

Water...trickling!

Picturing the Comfort Station, I ran toward it. Dense undergrowth pressed in on me. Branches reached out to scratch my face and scalp.

Suddenly the ground dropped away and I tripped and fell flat out across a tiny stream. I wasn't expecting that to happen and I didn't even have time to use my hands to break my fall. A large pointed rock stabbed me in the ribs and I heard a crack. It was the worst pain I'd ever felt. I wanted to throw up. I maybe even blacked out for a moment.

"Mom!" I screamed when I was finally able to get a big enough breath.

I forgot all about my firm resolve to not scream and I yelled "Help!" over and over until my voice was hoarse. In between I stopped to listen but no one heard me. No one came.

Then I had a horrible thought: *Mom won't even notice that I'm gone until the morning. No one will be looking for me before then.*

Curling up in a ball next to the stream, I pulled my hoodie over my head and hugged my aching ribs. I didn't want to. I tried to be brave but I couldn't help myself--I cried.

I should stay where I am, I thought. *Then my mom will find me.*

I shivered in fear and from being wet. Soon exhausted, I drifted in and out of a sleep that brought no rest. I dreamed of our visit earlier that day to the Algonquin Park Museum. I dreamed of the stuffed mother Black bear on display in the museum with her two taxidermal babies.

They weren't so big, I told myself.

Still, I wouldn't like to meet up with them.

"Hang your packs so bears can't get them," Dave had said. "Don't leave scraps around."

"If attacked, don't play dead. Fight back," the Park Naturalist had said.

I whimpered in a tormented half-sleep.

How could I have gotten myself in this situation? I wondered. *What are the chances that a bear will find me?*

I pictured what I would look like from a plane through infrared goggles. I'd be just a small, glowing dot on a huge landscape. I pictured my infrared dot and the dots that would represent wild animals in the park. I pictured those dots very far away from my dot. But this game brought no consolation.

Still, I shivered, cried and dreamed.

In my dream I was reliving being around the campfire earlier that evening with my mom and Dave.

"And then they found Tom Thomson's bloated and decomposing body days later floating face down in the water," Dave was saying.

He grimaced as he told the story, looking from me to my mother, his eyes wide and his fingers clawing the air for emphasis.

My mom's laugh echoed in my dream and the light from the campfire danced in her eyes.

Then I saw myself roll my eyes and look away from Dave. I was sulking and pretending not to listen to his story. I didn't want to go on this dumb camping trip and I was going to make my mom and Dave feel the pressure of my displeasure at every opportunity.

Still, there was something about the story of this famous Canadian painter that bothered me.

He was so young and talented. It doesn't sound like a canoeing accident to me, I thought in my dream.

Whatever happened it couldn't have been his fault. There had to be a bad guy.

Smashing his head on his own canoe and falling out is too ridiculous. Yes, Tom Thomson was definitely murdered, I thought, *by someone who was jealous of him.*

"Then," Dave was still talking, "the Thomson family hired a mortician to exhume his body and bring it back to Owen Sound to be buried in the family plot. So this creepy guy in a long black coat gets off at the Canoe Lake train station and goes up to the graveyard at night."

I dreamed of my mom. She was leaning forward as she listened to Dave's story. Her elbows were on her knees, her smiling face in her hands, her eyes shining.

"Come back in three hours, the mortician says. So three hours later the driver comes back and the mortician's done. Can you imagine?" Dave asked looking from me to my mom. "At night? Digging up a grave, pulling the rotting body out and putting it in another casket, then filling in the old grave all by yourself?"

In my dream I remembered that Dave howled like a wolf and reached over and grabbed my shoulder to make me jump.

It worked. I jumped but then pushed him away.

"It's so lame, Dave," I told him.

Dave laughed but it wasn't a real laugh. He was just trying to cover up how disappointed he was that we weren't close. It was the laugh of resignation.

I moaned and whimpered in my sleep. My dreams agitated me. The memory of my response to Dave haunted me as much as thoughts of Tom Thomson. I wrapped my arms around myself even tighter but couldn't stop myself from shivering.

"So then about twenty years later," Dave continued, "four guys decided to try to find the old grave of Tom Thomson. There was a rumour that Thomson's friends moved the body before the mortician got there and that the coffin was empty. So they go up in the middle of the night and start digging in the area. Well, they dug the first hole six feet down. Nothing. Then they picked another spot nearby and dug the second hole. Again, nothing. They dug a third hole and still nothing. They were just about to give up when one of them noticed a depression in the ground," he said, his eyes wide and dark.

"So they started digging, digging, digging and they hit wood! A coffin! 'There's something here!' one of them yelled. Then he saw that it was a box and the top was caved in. He could see a hole in the box. So he reaches down, down, down," Dave said reaching down into the imaginary coffin, "and he pulls out…"

Here Dave paused for emphasis.

Pulled out what?

"Down, down he reached and he pulled out a foot bone!"

"Eeewww," Mom shivered.

"So then, the four guys called the Ontario Provincial Police because the coffin was supposed to be empty. And the OPP did some tests and they discovered that it wasn't Tom Thomson's body! It was someone else! It was the body of a native man!

So how did the body of another man get in Tom Thomson's grave?"

I just shrugged my indifference but the truth is that I couldn't stop thinking about it.

Something funny was definitely going on.

"And all this happened right here in Algonquin Park," Dave concluded.

"How far away?" I had to know.

"It's just the next lake over, on Canoe Lake."

"So you brought us camping to a murder scene?"

"Well it did happen almost a hundred years ago. Although," he said lowering his voice, "they say his spirit still roams the park. Listen to this part of the story: someone who said he knew where Thomson's friends moved the body was about to show everyone the spot when he died in a fluke accident. He was crossing Canoe Lake in the winter, dragging supplies in a sled behind him when he broke through the ice on the exact spot where Tom Thomson's body was found! So what do you think of that, M.E.?"

Wow, Algonquin Park is haunted--cool, I remembered thinking but instead I just rolled my eyes as if Dave's story was the greatest bore and said, "Lame."

It was the "final straw" as they say.

"That's enough!" my mom said and jumped to her feet.

I knew I'd touched a nerve. My rudeness and eye rolling had been piling up on top of my refusal to like or even accept Dave.

"It's just rude! Apologize right now!"

"What for?" I shouted back.

"Mary Elizabeth!"

"Okay, just forget it!" I remembered yelling. I stormed off toward the tent. I figured if I yelled back my mother would be stunned just long enough for me to make it back to the tent before being forced to apologize.

It worked.

I remembered thinking about running away as I stomped off.

But at the moment, running away was such a repulsive thought that it jolted me out of my dream. Shivering on the ground, clutching my fractured rib, itchy and bleeding, my only thought was that I wished I was still sleeping in my warm tent next to my mom and Dave—even if he did snore like a jackhammer.

"Mom!" I cried.

I'd never felt so sorry for myself in my life. Then a dreamless sleep mercifully carried me to the dawn of the next day.

Chapter 3

I bolted awake with the morning light.

"Mom!" was my first thought.

A fierce stab of pain pierced my ribs and I could hardly get up.

The truth of my situation washed over me but overhead a cacophony of chirping, cheeping, cawing, and squawking announced the start of a new day.

I staggered to my feet and looked in every direction. Nothing was familiar. There was no sign of the campground or the Comfort Station. There was no sign of civilization whatsoever.

"Hello!" I yelled. "Help me!"

There was no reply. I listened hard to hear any human or man-made sound. There was nothing.

Wait! What's that?

A *tock-tock-tock* filled me with hope. It sounded like a hammer tapping lightly. Maybe it was a workman fixing something.

Maybe he has a truck with a two-way radio. But high up a tree I spotted a woodpecker pecking at a hole-filled trunk. I could see a red patch of feathers on the back of its head. Then it flitted to another tree calling *ki-ki-ki-ki-ki* and my hopeful vision of a worker flew off with it.

"Hello!" I yelled again. "Is anybody there? Anybody?"

I strained to hear or see anything. But there was nothing except the wind and trees in every direction. Still damp from falling into the creek the night before and from the dew, I hugged myself to try to quell my violent shivering. Then, scooping some water from the cold creek, I took a little drink.

The spot on my ribs ached. I lifted my hoodie to have a look. An ugly purple bruise had formed. I touched it tenderly. It felt painful beyond belief.

It's broken. It feels like it's broken. I gotta get outta here. What am I gonna do? What am I gonna do?

I looked up and down the creek but one direction looked exactly like the other.

I should follow this creek. It must come out somewhere.

The forest seemed full of birds this morning, each one warbling a happy song. It was annoying.

A Gray Jay landed on a nearby branch. *Whee-ah, whu-whu-whu* it sang fluffing its gray wings and white belly feathers before it shot off to another tree.

If I follow the creek, it must come out somewhere.

I stumbled along beside the creek ducking under branches and climbing over rocks. The creek snaked its way along the lowest crevices of land.

"It has to come out somewhere," I kept repeating out loud.

Then, climbing over baseball-sized rocks that clacked like billiard balls, I turned my ankle and cried out in pain. Tears poured down my cheeks.

I'm okay. I'm okay, I thought as I rubbed my ankle and rotated it.

It's not broken, I told myself yet tears of self-pity poured down my cheeks.

I forced myself to continue following the creek.

I gotta keep going. This creek has gotta come out somewhere.

After a couple of hours I noticed that the trees in this part of the forest were different from the ones that surrounded me that morning. Now it was mostly spruce trees.

The squawking of birds seemed to get louder. Suddenly I came upon a circular opening in the forest. It wasn't man-made. There were no tree stumps. It was just a sunny area clear of trees. Short grasses and moss or something like lichen covered the area.

Bizarre. It's like a crop circle.

Stepping out of the shade of the forest, I felt warmer. I lifted my face to the sun to take in the warmth. I noticed steam lifting off my damp hoodie sleeve as the sun evaporated the moisture.

The ground underfoot was soft and springy like a waterbed.

This is a bog, I realized.

I remembered the Park Naturalist describing bogs to us on our museum tour. I looked around. Sure enough, sphagnum mosses, sedge and Labrador tea bushes grew around the edge. I took a step and felt the ground bounce back. Black spruce trees stood like sentinels around the edge of this springy meadow. They let off a faint menthol smell. Most of the spruce trees were grey and dead-looking at the bottom but the top six feet or so were green and healthy.

I jumped on the bouncy turf a couple more times and noticed that it caused a slow ripple that spread out from where I jumped in an ever-widening circle.

It's so strange, was my last thought before my leg burst through right up to my hip.

"No!" I shrieked.

I felt angry at myself for being so dumb and also horrified at the thought of getting sucked into the bog.

Grasping fists full of moss, I pulled myself out. The bog made a sucking sound as it slowly released me. Not daring to stand on it again, I crawled on my hands and knees toward the spruce trees. Black muck covered my entire leg and the sliminess of it freaked me out as much as breaking through the bog mat.

Crying and scared, I dragged my leg along the ground to try to scrape off the slimy black mud. When my flannel pyjama bottoms were as clean as I could get them I stretched out on the ground and had a good cry.

Another good cry! Normally I would've felt like the greatest wuss but in this situation it never crossed my mind.

"Someone help me!" I cried with a growing sense of futility.

I remembered visiting the Bog People exhibit at the Museum of Civilization in Ottawa. I learned that during the Iron Age the Celts sometimes threw people into bogs as human sacrifices. When they were found almost a thousand years later they were perfectly preserved like a black Chinese century egg. Their skin and hair was still intact but the acid in the peat dissolved the calcium carbonate in their bones and they looked like empty pieces of black leather luggage.

I hated that exhibit. I had nightmares about bog people for months. I shuddered at the thought of getting sucked into the black mud and becoming a bog person. I pictured myself on display in a museum exhibit with a flattened inky hide.

What if Mom thinks I've run away? She may not be looking for me at all!

I remembered complaining about camping on the way to Algonquin Park just as we passed a hitchhiker on the road.

"I could hitchhike home," I said nonchalantly baiting the hook.

"Oh, no you won't!" I remember my mom snapping at the bait. "Don't you understand how dangerous that is? You never get into a car with a stranger! You'd be making yourself vulnerable. Plus, you'd be trapped. No one does that anymore because everyone knows how dangerous it is!"

What if Mom thinks I ignored her advice and hitchhiked back to Toronto?

I tried to shake the thought from my mind and replace it with something positive but it was impossible.

To distract myself, I gathered a handful of small twigs and arranged them so that they spelled out my initials, ME, on the edge of the clearing.

If someone passes by at least they'll know that I was here.

A chipmunk trilled at me from the branches of a tree. I looked up. It was definitely "talking" to me. The chipmunk looked right at me as it scolded in its high-pitched voice.

"What do you want?" I asked it.

Its piercing chatter alarmed me. It set my nerves on edge.

I watched the little creature scramble down the tree then dive head first into a tiny, hole hidden in the ground. In a moment, it was out again darting here and there, its tail twitching spastically all the while angrily scolding me.

I watched it dig at the base of a tree and pluck out a maple key then it darted back into its underground burrow. I thought about how warm and snug the chipmunk's burrow must be.

"Some people like to sleep right out under the stars," Dave had said as he unrolled our tent, "but not me. You need at least a ground sheet and a tarp of some sort over your head to keep the dew off."

I thought how odd it was that these snippets of advice Dave had given when I wasn't really listening would come back to me now. I decided that I would try to build some kind of shelter for myself tonight if I didn't find my way back before then.

Noticing that the mud on my pyjama bottoms was drying I decided it was time to keep moving so I circled around the outside edge of the bog.

Walking in the warm sun, two dragonflies circled over my head. One landed on my shoulder. I was worried that it would bite me and I swatted it away. But it circled in the air and landed on my head.

"Stop!" I cried waving my hands frantically and it flew off.

But the dragonflies would not be put off and one of them again attempted a landing. As it got close I watched it snatch a mosquito right out of the air.

Wow, it eats mosquitoes!

As it hovered near me I admired its perfectly transparent wings and dusty blue body.

It's beautiful. Maybe they don't bite, I told myself.

I held out the back of my hand and to my surprise the dragonfly landed on it. I examined it more carefully but found no evidence of a stinger or a proboscis. The dragonfly settled and made no attempt to bite me. Then the second dragonfly landed on my shoulder and suddenly I felt grateful for the company.

I gotta get outta here. Which way?

I scanned the edge of the bog. There was nothing to give me any indication of the direction I should take. I continued circling around the outside edge to where the bog mat opened up and found a stream coming out the other side.

Maybe I should continue following this creek.

"We're following this creek, okay guys? Is that a good idea?" I asked the dragonflies.

At least I'll have water, I thought as I set out.

"Always pack a bottle of drinking water and some matches when you go hiking," I remembered Dave saying.

Well that's all very well if you're planning on hiking. But in my case...

The creek led me away from the sunny bog and back into dense forest. I felt the drop in temperature immediately and so did the dragonflies which lifted off and flew back toward the sunshine.

"Hey, where are you going?" I felt abandoned. "Wait!"

I waited to see if they'd come back but soon lost sight of them so I continued on my way.

After walking only a kilometre or two I noticed that the creek was cutting deeper creating a bank on either side. Soon I became aware of the sound of crashing, tumbling water and I realized that the creek was leading me to some other body of water. Excited, I quickened my pace.

Through the trees I could see that the creek spilled into a wide, racing river that cut through a canyon. There was no sign of life in either direction.

Which way? Which way?

On my side of the river a granite cliff stretched up three hundred feet. At the top I could see Red-Tailed hawks swirling and landing on precarious ledges to tend to their nests.

Watching them circle so high in the sky I thought, *if I could get to the top of that cliff I'd be able to see all the way to the highway and to the campgrounds.*

So I began the gruelling climb to the top of the cliff.

My stomach never gave me a moment's rest.

I'm starving! I gotta have food, I thought.

My stomach nagged at me. It produced images of pizza and tacos. I tried to push those pictures out of my mind so that I could concentrate on the climb but it was hopeless. I kept my eyes on the hawks.

When I get to the top I'll be able to see my campsite and figure out which way to go.

I watched three or four hawks circle on the updrafts without flapping. With wings outstretched, wingtips upturned, they made big circles in the sky. They seemed to float so effortlessly. They looked as though they were just having fun but, in fact, their sharp black eyes scanned the river shore and forest edge for any sign of prey.

At times the tree branches were so tightly intertwined that I had to stop and search for a way through. Underfoot gnarled roots threatened to trip my every step.

Every few metres of my climb I stopped to look at the lowering horizon but saw only dense forest for as far as the eye could see. As the sun began to set I climbed faster, desperate to get to the top.

I wanna go home. I wanna go home.

But the darker it got the more difficult it became to see exactly where I was placing my foot.

Suddenly my right foot settled on a loose rock that broke away and I dropped onto one knee. Screaming, my arms flung out in front of me, fingers outstretched, reaching, and grasping at the air. I caught hold of a thin tree root with my right hand. My right leg flew out over the edge of the cliff desperately searching for a foothold.

I'm gonna die!

Just as the tree root in my right hand broke off, my left hand caught a branch.

Somewhere behind me I could hear the loud, descending scream *keeer-r-r, keeer-r-r* of the hawks. I held on with my left hand as best I could in my weakened state while my right hand reached and grabbed wildly at the air. My foot hunted for a toehold but everywhere it landed the stones crumbled and fell away. Down the side of the craggy cliff they bounced until the rushing river swallowed them up.

Chapter 4

Throwing my weight forward a stab of pain jolted through my whole body but I squeezed the branch tighter. I moved my hand further up the branch and grabbed a fistful of turf with my right.

I held. I wasn't slipping.

I can't stay like this!

I knew what I had to do.

There's no other way!

I had no choice. And so with a burst of courage and energy, I swung my right leg over the edge and slid my left hand further up the branch. As my feet scrambled behind me they dislodged more stones that broke off and fell into the chasm below. I inched forward on my stomach ever so carefully until my entire abdomen was back on the cliff. The pain in my fractured rib was excruciating but I made it!

Once on my feet, I clung to the nearest substantial tree trunk. I was out of danger but I wanted to grab onto something sturdy while I clutched my ribs and bawled ferociously.

That was so freaking close! I shuddered. *I'm really in trouble! What am I gonna do?*

With the crash of the water below added to my own blubbering, I didn't hear the sound of beating blades approaching until the helicopter passed directly overhead.

"Wait!" I yelled clambering along the cliff edge trying to find a break in the dense foliage so I could show myself.

The helicopter banked to the right so that it could get a better view of the river. I could see the letters OPP on the bottom.

"Wait!" I yelled again. "I'm here! Over here!"

I waved my arms and scrambled along the precipice but could not make myself get too near the edge after such a close call.

"Help! Help! I'm over here!" I screamed but my voice was lost under the roar of the engine.

The helicopter continued following the river and in no time at all it was a tiny speck on the darkening horizon just as I came out on a clearing at the apex of the cliff.

"Wait! Come back!" I screamed jumping and waving until I could neither hear it nor see it anymore.

At least they're looking for me, I thought with a lump in my throat.

"Mom knows I didn't run away," I said out loud and big tears of relief rolled down my cheeks. "Mom knows!"

Maybe the helicopter will come back.

I was now directly above the spot in the cliff where the hawks were nesting. Instead of looking up at their cream-coloured undersides I was now looking down on their brown mottled backs and wings.

It's so weird to look down on birds in flight, I thought as I watched them swoop out and circle a couple of times below me.

Keeer-r-r, keeer-r-r their cry echoed off the trees.

Pink melted into turquoise in the western sky as the sun, a huge, piercing, orange ball, fell over the horizon. It was a Tom Thomson landscape: pristine lakes, rolling hills thick with trees, and puffy clouds scudding across the horizon.

I glanced at it but only noticed that it was getting dark. I tossed about for something I could use as a shelter. There wasn't much up there--just one lone Jack Pine, bare rock and some low-growing brush.

I wonder if this is the Jack Pine Tom Thomson painted, I thought picturing the painting I had seen in a museum.

"It represents isolation and the struggle to survive against the elements in the harsh Canadian landscape," I remembered overhearing one museum visitor saying to another as they stood fixed on the famous Thomson painting.

Examining the shrubs more closely, I noticed that they were covered in dull, dark berries. I picked one and sniffed it.

It looks like a blueberry but what if it's poison?

I had only ever eaten blueberries in a pie and a cooked blueberry looks and tastes very different from a fresh blueberry. I was so hungry. I tore off the tiniest bit of peel and pinched it between my front teeth.

These are definitely blueberries!

I popped it in my mouth and chomped almost without tasting while I scoured the bushes for more. There were lots but the sun had set and I had only a few minutes to find them. When I couldn't see them anymore I found them with my fingers and gorged myself until my grumbling stomach quieted a little.

After that, I brushed away some loose rubble and lay with my back against a layer of rock under the towering Jack Pine.

Taking a small stone I scratched out my initials ME on the rocky ledge.

Pulling the hood of my fleece up over my head, I fell back and stared at the big sky. The peach sunset was gone—replaced by an ever-deepening azure that gave way to complete darkness. I had never seen so many stars. They occupied every corner of the night sky. Suddenly a shooting star streaked from one horizon to the other.

Seeing a shooting star is supposed to be good luck. I could make a wish.

I wish I may, I wish I might, have the wish I wish tonight. I wish that I wasn't lost. I wish that someone will find me. I wish that I will be able to see my mother—soon.

I spotted several other falling stars but I was exhausted and soon fell into a fitful sleep. I half-dreamed of, half-remembered again, my visit to the Bog People exhibit.

I was leaning on a wall in the museum and drawing a big gothic M in black marker on the back of my hand.

"Can we go now?" I asked my mother with as much attitude as someone could squeeze into four short words.

"There's no rush," I remembered my mother saying with forced cheerfulness. "We just got here. We're going to have a little lunch and then we'll see the Group of Seven exhibit."

"I wanna go shopping," I said completing the initial E on the back of my hand.

I knew initials should be separated by periods but I always left them out because I liked it that my initials spelled "me".

"I can't really afford any more shopping this month, M.E.," my mother said.

"Let's get outta here," I whined. "I wanna go shopping."

Then I remembered my mother's face—a slow-burning ember that burst into full flame.

"It's always all about me, me, me isn't it?" my mother hissed. "Well, I have news: it's not always about you!"

The memory of my mother's frustration was so tangible that I could almost taste it, smell it. I remembered that I didn't respond to the remark but in my mind I thought, *yeah, it IS all about me.*

After that I dreamed that I got my wish to shop. Stepping out of a clothing store change room I stood in front of the mirror wearing a black shorty dress.

In my dream I recoiled at my reflection.

I look like a bog person! I thought, horrified.

Then a distant howling and my eyes shot open.

Wolves!

I strained to see, to hear. The Jack Pine trembled in the wind. The wolves repeated their plaintive cry.

They're far away! They're far away! I told myself as convincingly as I could.

A long *woo-oo-ooo* and many more drifted through the air and bounced off the cliff where I lay. I couldn't tell exactly where the howling was coming from—behind me in the woods or somewhere in the forest at the bottom of the cliff.

"The pack howls so that they can identify each other over long distances and stay together," I remembered the Park Naturalist saying.

Several wolf pups joined in the howling. Their adolescent voices broke into yipping and yelping.

I hated that sound. I plugged my ears, squeezed my eyes shut and turned my head away. I was stuck in the surreal world between the wolves howling in my wakefulness and the bog people in my dream. Neither was appealing.

I shivered from cold and out of fear of the wolves. I tried to think of something else but all that came to my mind was my fight with my mom outside the Bog People exhibit.

I ruined the day with my mom, I thought. *I ruined it.*

I hugged my fractured rib and shivered under my hood with my back to the cold, exposed rock. I remembered hearing my mother and Dave whispering around the campfire after I'd stomped off.

"She'll come around," Dave had said. "It's hard for kids to accept a new man in their mom's life."

"I'm sure you're right," my mother said.

I resolved to be nice to my mother. I resolved to apologize.

If I ever get the chance, I thought with a sob.

Chapter 5

In the morning of the second day, I woke and immediately remembered the little dusty indigo berries. Now that I had light, I could pick the bushes clean and eat my fill. When I could eat no more I filled my pockets until there were no blueberries left.

This accomplished two things. First, I felt physically better. I felt revived. Also, I felt better emotionally because I had the sense of having stocked up for my journey back home.

I approached the edge of the cliff. From that lofty height the view was magnificent but I was in no mood to appreciate it.

This park is huge! It goes on forever! Where's the highway? I can't be that far from the highway.

I studied the rolling hills on the distant horizon for any sign of civilization but I saw only trees for ten kilometres in every direction: pine, maple, cedar and spruce broken up by the occasional deep blue lake.

Where is everyone?

I could see no roads snaking through the trees, no motorboats on the shimmering lakes, not even a plane in the sky.

"Hellooooo," I shouted but my words only echoed back at me.

Then, about 500 metres down the river, I spotted two men in a green canoe. With some difficulty they hauled their canoe onto the shore on the opposite side of the river near a small dark cabin almost hidden from view.

"Hello! Hello!" I screamed waving my arms wildly. "Over here! I'm over here!"

But the men didn't look up.

They can't hear me over the noise of the river.

I began running along the edge of the cliff. Going down was nearly as hard as the climb up the day before. My breath came in whining gasps.

"Wait! Wait! I'm here!"

I watched them jump out of the canoe. They wore matching uniforms.

They're Park Naturalists! I thought. *They're looking for me!*

"Wait!" I cried as I stumbled over rocks and roots and ducked under and around branches.

I saw one go into the cabin and the other walked around the outside.

"Help!" I screamed holding one hand over my tender, fractured rib.

The one on the inside reappeared and the two men discussed something for a moment as they looked up and down the river. They didn't see me. I was hidden by the trees.

"Wait!" I shouted scrambling over low growing brush and loose rubble.

Then I almost lost my footing again and memories of the terror of the night before convinced me to take care.

"Wait!" I cried fighting my way through the brush. I clawed open a break in the trees.

By that time, the Park Naturalists were climbing back into their canoe.

"No, wait!" I cried with a desperate, sinking feeling because I knew they still could not hear me since I wasn't yet even halfway down the cliff.

I continued stumbling downward but I knew it was hopeless.

"Wait!" I wailed as I watched them push off into the river. "I'm here! I'm here!"

Then the swift current grabbed their canoe and swept it away. I watched them not so much paddle as steer. Soon they were only a shrinking spot of green on the river.

Onward I continued my reckless descent but by the time I got to the river's edge they were gone. Bent over with hands on knees I tried to catch my breath, still my racing heart and warm my icy lungs. I stumbled along the river in the direction the Park Naturalists had taken. River rocks clacked under my feet. Tears streamed down my face.

First I missed the helicopter and now I've missed the Park Naturalists. How many more chances will I get?

After a while I rounded a bend and caught sight of the one-room cabin on the opposite side of the river.

Maybe there's a phone and food, I thought noticing my hunger.

Then, remembering my stash of berries, I dug into my pocket but found only pulp. I had crushed them all with my fall. Still, I scooped out the pulp with my fingernails and ate all that I could.

When I was directly across the river from the cabin I pulled my hood up over my head and tied it by the arms around my waist with a double knot. Then I launched myself into the water with strong strokes.

The current fought against me but I was a good swimmer. I clenched my teeth and continued stroking. I thought about the years of swimming lessons my mother insisted I take and felt grateful for every one of them.

But before I was even a third of the way, I felt the current overpowering me, pulling at my waterlogged clothes. My legs shot up behind me and my head went under.

This was a bad idea.

I twisted and rolled. When I opened my eyes underwater, I could see only swirling bubbles and detritus. My long hair whipped around and across my eyes. Disoriented, I swam for the surface but hit the bottom. I thought my lungs would burst. Over and around I rolled. With lungs stretched and straining, I shot off in another direction. Finally, my head bobbed to the surface in time to take a huge gasp of air. Then my back slammed into a large rock and nearly knocked that gasp of air right out of me. Facing backwards, I lost sight of the little cabin as I was swept around a bend in the river.

Is this the end?

Then I thought of the famous painter.

I'm gonna drown in Algonquin Park just like Tom Thomson! I thought.

I struggled to turn myself around and stay above the surface so I could at least see where I was going. But no matter how much I flailed I made no headway.

This was a mistake!

I was helpless to control my body that bobbed and dunked like a cork. I got pulled under again but this time my feet hit the bottom right away and I knew that the river was shallower at this point.

Pushing myself to the surface, I caught another breath just in time to see that I was racing out of control toward another huge rock.

Chapter 6

Crashing into the rock was unavoidable but this time I was ready. I latched onto it with a strong grip and, even though my legs whipped around, I didn't let go. Hugging both arms around the rock I inched my way to the other side, willing myself to hold on.

This was a mistake, I thought. *The current is way stronger than I thought. I'll never get to the other side.*

About five metres down river and closer to the side I started from, I spotted another large rock jutting out of the water. Pushing off with my arms outstretched I was able to propel myself about ten feet closer to shore, but still I missed the rock. My fingertips only just brushed it as the current pulled me past.

I'm getting closer to shore!

I cut through the water as best I could until I hit the shallows on the same side of the river where I started.

Staggering out of the water, I collapsed on the riverbank.

How can I get to the other side?

Waves of self-pity washed over my sodden body. My situation seemed so hopeless.

I lay on the rocky riverbank until I caught my breath.

What am I gonna do?

My hand rested on a smooth oval stone. I picked it up and rolled it over. It was beautiful. Specks in the granite reflected the sunlight. Next I spotted a quartz stone. It looked like cloudy glass. Then I found a striped stone and a red oxide one.

They're beautiful, I thought.

"You're beautiful," I remembered my mother telling me. "Look at you with your beautiful shiny hair. You don't need makeup. You have natural beauty. And anyway, your body is just a shell. The real you is on the inside."

How many other nice things had my mother said to me over the years? Countless things, I thought.

My mother always found a way to compliment me.

The real me on the inside isn't so nice, I thought and for the thousandth time good intentions danced on the edge of my mind.

I pocketed the four stones and lined up other stones on the shore so that they spelled ME. My obsession with my initials became a need to mark my whereabouts; to leave a trail.

When I finished, I untied my hoodie and wrung it out. Then I took off my shirt and pyjama bottoms and wrung them out.

I took a moment to examine my bruised rib. It was an unnatural deep purple in the centre with green patches around the outside.

Hearing a rustle in the trees, I looked up to see a family of White-tailed deer: a buck, a doe and a faun. When they spotted me they froze and stared with wide, unblinking eyes. They directed their ears at me like six little satellite dishes. I stood motionless watching them.

Wow, it's magical!

After a couple of minutes the doe bent her head to nibble at a bush. Suddenly, as if suspecting foul play, she snapped it back to give me another long, hard stare.

How silly. Do I look like a hunter? I smiled to myself.

Meanwhile, like all youngsters, the faun was less patient with this game of "Freeze". It brushed against its mother and walked around to her other side so it could suckle. I noticed their long, skinny necks and legs and their relatively small heads. If they were playing a real game of Freeze, the buck would have won hooves-down. He didn't move even a millimetre.

I watched the faun suckle for a while.

At least it has its mother, I thought.

When the doe moved the faun followed, pushing its way under its mother so that it could latch on again from a new position. It was demanding, relentless, focused on its own needs, oblivious to the danger I might pose, oblivious to the bother it caused its mother.

I'm glad I'm not a mother deer, I thought. *I'd hate to have someone push me around like that. It's so demanding, so selfish.*

Then I thought about me, pushing my mother as much as I dared, demanding money for clothes, thinking only about myself.

I hated thinking these thoughts. They made me feel uncomfortable. I tried to shake them from my mind but they haunted me.

I gotta get outta here.

The current had pulled me about a half kilometre past the cabin and I was still on the opposite side.

There's no point following the Park Naturalists. I'll never catch them.

I set off following the river in the direction from which the Naturalists had come.

As soon as I took a step, the family of deer bolted into the bush. Looking up, I saw their long white tails sway from side to side and then they were gone.

I'm so hungry. I need food, I thought as I trudged along.

My wet pyjama bottoms dragged at me but luckily the sun was strong and they were slowly drying out. Half an hour later, I passed the cabin. There it was looking empty and dark.

There is shelter right there—how stupid that I can't even get to it!

I kept going. After a while, I could see why the current was so strong. The river was flowing downhill and it was quite narrow at the top. At the highest, narrowest part the river was blocked by fallen logs and a jumble of branches. When I got to the top of the hill I could see that it was blocked by a beaver dam and on the other side of it was a large pond.

I scooped up some water to drink.

So now I had a decision to make. If I continued on I may come to a ranger station or I could cross over the dam to the opposite side of the river and backtrack half a kilometre to the cabin. Then at least I'd have shelter for the night.

Those Park Naturalists could have travelled ten kilometres to get here.

Somehow the cabin seemed like a surer thing.

Maybe another couple of Naturalists will canoe by, I thought hopefully.

But walking across the top of a beaver dam is one thing in theory and it's another thing doing it.

Will it hold my weight?

It looked like a loose pile of sticks and mud. I pressed it with my hands. It was as solid as if it was made out of cement. I pushed it with my foot. It didn't even budge. I climbed on and bounced a little but it was rock solid. Memories of breaking through the bog mat were at the forefront of my mind.

What if it caves in when I'm halfway across?

But the beaver dam was even sturdier than I could have hoped. Nevertheless, I stepped cautiously because, solid or not, it was still made up of a jumble of branches, each one gnawed to a point and jutting dangerously in every direction.

When I was less than halfway across, I heard a loud splash in the water and looked up to see a beaver lodge only a few metres away. To me it seemed like nothing more than a heap of branches and twigs. I couldn't see that most of the lodge was actually under water. Next to the lodge I noticed ripples in the pond heading straight toward me at an alarming speed. My heart jumped into my throat.

The beaver is coming!

I felt like a trespasser on a construction site.

I watched the swell in the water getting closer. My heart raced. Then, only a couple of metres away, the beaver surfaced. It looked me over. It was obviously not afraid of me.

Should I be afraid of him? I wondered. *Do beaver bite?*

I remembered seeing curved, dark orange beaver teeth on display somewhere.

Another beaver, a smaller one, appeared next to the first one. I was surprised by their size. The big one blinked at me. Then it slapped its tail on the surface of the water and dove under. I jumped at the loud clap and lost my balance. I fell forward on one knee and a pointed stick gouged my shin.

"My leg!"

I rushed off the beaver dam as fast as I could. When I got to the other side, I bent to examine my leg. Blood soaked into my sock. I pressed a large leaf over my wound and checked it several times. Tears poured down my cheeks.

First my ribs and now my leg!

Glancing back, I could see no sign of the beavers. I limped along the edge of the pond toward the mouth of the river. My only thought was to get to the cabin.

If I get to the cabin everything will be all right, I thought. *Maybe there's food. Maybe I'll find some bandages.*

I caught sight of the squat, dark cabin just as the sun was setting. Set back a little from the river, it was almost hidden by the overgrown trees.

I wonder if this was Tom Thomson's cabin.

"Hello," I called. "Is anybody there?"

All thoughts of a warm, welcoming shelter were overshadowed by my first sight of the foreboding shack.

"Hello," I called but the word caught in my throat and presented as little more than a tremulous whisper.

"Hello," I called more boldly.

Nothing. Just the wind in the tree tops.

With night closing in I willed myself up the dilapidated steps. Signs of abandonment were everywhere: the curled wooden siding, a broken plank on the porch, the screen door hung on one hinge, mould grew thick on the roof shingles.

The blood on my leg had dried by then but I had forgotten about it. My pain was of far less importance than the idea of spending another night outside.

I pushed open the battered door.

"Hello."

Nothing. I stared into the blackness and listened but I could see nothing and could hear nothing. It was so dark I could only make out a counter along one wall. Tiny shoots of plants and fungus grew out of the floorboards. Piles of animal feces covered the entire floor. As my eyes adjusted I could see a broken tea cup, shredded newspaper, and an overturned kitchen chair.

"Hello."

When my eyes adjusted as well as they would to the gloomy interior, I could see a table and a very foul smelling cot along one wall. I stepped into the middle of the room. Stuffing ripped from the cot was gathered in a corner under the bed.

There's no way I'm sleeping on that bed, I thought.

Most of the cupboards over the counter hung open. There was nothing. The thought that this could be Tom Thomson's cabin kept coming back to me. Ghost stories about haunted houses filled my mind.

It began to rain.

I sat in the open door staring out at the rain. I hated having all that gloomy cabin interior at my back but I hated sitting inside the dark cabin even more.

I felt for the four stones in my pocket. Rolling them over in my hand I realized I could tell them apart by feel. The oval granite one I could tell by its perfect oval shape. The jagged edges of the quartz stone identified it. The red oxide stone was pitted and I could feel the ridges on the striped one.

My stomach churned and growled. I remembered when Dave took me to lunch at a popular deli near our house. It was a snowy Saturday. The place was packed with happy customers jostling and joking and stamping the snow off their shoes. It was sort of a getting-to-know-you-better lunch. Dave handed me a plate with a hot Montreal smoked meat sandwich and a sizeable garlic pickle. It was the best sandwich I'd ever tasted. My mouth watered now thinking about it.

"It's good, eh?" Dave asked watching me.

"It's okay," I lied trying to seem underwhelmed.

Remembering this, a tear dropped from my eye. A half-formed intention came to me that had to do with changing some things when I get home.

The wind whipped up and blew in. I closed the door but not all the way. My bowels cramped. I lay behind the door with my face at the opening in an effort to block out the putrid smell in the cabin.

It's disgusting in here, I thought.

"It's disgusting in here," I remembered my mother saying to me with hands on hips as she surveyed my bedroom.

My closet overflowed with shoes I never wore and clothes I never bothered to hang up. Rolled up socks, hair brushes and bracelets poked out from under my bed. Candy wrappers, nail polish and more clothes littered the floor. Mom called my room a "floordrobe".

Ha ha. So funny. Why did I always argue with my Mom about my room? Why didn't I just clean it up?

I fell asleep on the hard cabin floor picturing my warm bed, the thick carpet and the bottles of flowery body mist I kept on my dresser.

Then I remembered my mother at my bedroom door when I was sick.

"I brought you a cup of tea," she smiled. "Are you feeling better?"

The memory of that moment brought fresh tears to my eyes.

I tried to ignore the lump in my throat. All I wanted was for sleep to do away with the night.

Now I lay me down to sleep...

Sometime later that night a loud bang woke me with a start. My eyes darted all around.

"What? Who's there?"

A second bang. A third. It was coming from outside. A fourth bang. A fifth. A sixth.

It's the wind.

A seventh bang. The wind had caught a shutter and was banging it on the side of the house. Outside the rain continued to pour down.

Suddenly my bowels cramped and I ran outside to relieve myself.

Was it the blueberries? Was it the water I drank near the beaver pond?

Four times I returned to the cabin only to have to run back outside again. I washed myself in the river before returning to the foul cabin.

When my bowels finally settled I lay back down behind the door. Just as I began to drift off I became aware of the lightest scratching and scuffling coming from somewhere across the room.

What was that? I thought, my eyes wide.

Again the spectre of Tom Thomson filled my mind and I strained to see something in the inky corners of the dark cabin. But there was nothing.

There's no such thing as ghosts. There's no such thing as ghosts, I chanted as I forced myself to lie back down.

Suddenly I felt something on my hair. I shrieked, bolted upright and swatted at it. I was thinking spider and was therefore all the more surprised when my hand grabbed at a small mouse on my head.

It was in my hand and I screamed and flung it across the room. It hit something with a dull thud and fell to the floor.

What was that? It was a mouse! I think it was a mouse! Oh my gosh, I think I killed it!

I didn't know which was worse, the thought that I might have killed a little mouse or the realization that a mouse was in my hair--my beautiful, shiny, hair!

If I did kill it, it was an accident, I told myself.

I hated rodents. I could never bring myself to hold my neighbour's pet gerbil or even touch the guinea pig my grade two teacher kept in a cage at the back of the class. When I was ten and my friend Eddy lifted his sweater to show me his pet rat, I took one look at its long pink tail and screeched so loud that Eddy dropped it and it escaped. Eddy called me a dumb girl and we were never very good friends after that.

Presently I heard light scratching again and hoped that it meant that "my" mouse was okay. I lay with one arm looped up over my head protectively and the other draped over my neck.

Mice don't bite, I kept telling myself. *Mice don't bite. They're harmless. Some people think they're cute. If I ever get home, I'll clean up my room without fighting with my mom.*

Chapter 7

In the morning the rain had stopped. A thick mist filled in the spaces between the birch trees and gave the woods an otherworldly, claustrophobic feel.

I felt weak and dehydrated from all the times in the night I ran outside to relieve myself. I was feverish from having slept in wet clothes. I forced myself to think.

What should I do? Should I wait here and hope the Park Naturalists come back? Should I keep walking? But it looks so spooky out there in the fog. What should I do?

I sat up and winced in pain. Lifting my sweater, I examined the bruise that by now was a sickening colour of green.

What would Mom say if she saw that? I wondered.

Looking around the cabin, I dismissed the thought that this could have been Tom Thomson's cabin.

There was no sign that an artist had ever lived there. This was not an artistic mess. There was nothing special about this chaos. It was just a mess caused by exposure to the elements, maybe some people nosing around in here, breaking the windows and leaving a mess behind. Plus obviously some wild animals had been inside.

Unfortunately, there was no phone, no food, no bandages and no matches. There was nothing useful here at all—except shelter.

Then I set right a chair and spotted a fishing knife. It was heavier than I expected. It had a curved blade and a heavy white ivory handle with steel rivets.

Picking up the knife, I absently carved ME into the cabin floor in the doorway.

What should I do? What should I do? Should I stay here or keep going?

I brushed aside the shavings and looked at my initials for a very long time. Finally, I bent over again and took the time to put periods in between the letters.

"Mary Elizabeth," I said aloud. "It's not about me."

What should I do?

I stared out at the thick, spooky fog.

If I get out there in the middle of it I could really get lost, I thought.

What should I do? I should go. I can hear the river. It's straight ahead. I'm going, I decided willing myself to move.

Guided by the sound of the rushing river, I walked through the swirling mist toward it.

If I didn't have the river to follow, I thought, *I'd really be lost.*

The damp and earthy smell of the woods filled my head.

It's so quiet. Except for the river, it's so quiet.

I could not see more than three metres in any direction. A white haze closed in around me. Spooked, I fingered the knife in my hoodie pocket.

It's the birds. That's why it's so quiet. I don't hear any birds.

Pushing through the dense undergrowth my pyjama bottoms were soon soaked again and clinging to my legs. When I reached the riverbank just a few metres away I looked back toward the cabin but it was gone; swallowed by the eerie vapour that rolled and coiled between the tree trunks.

There must be something just past the beaver dam, I reasoned as I stumbled along the riverbank. *There must be a campground, a trail—something. If I get past the beaver dam and find nothing I'll turn around and follow the river back to the cabin.*

Though wet and shivering with a fever and out of fear, I pressed on through the thick mist beside the river. I felt closed in—claustrophobic—as if the trees were pressing in on me.

What if I'm only going deeper into the park? What if this river is taking me deeper in and farther away from my mom's campsite?

I felt weak and light-headed. I pictured my own stomach a small, empty space.

I have to have food! There must be more blueberries somewhere, I thought scouring the bushes as I walked.

Blueberries were the only bit of food I'd eaten for days. I spotted a young fern still tightly wound and close to the ground. Drops of water ran off the pale green shoot. I stopped to get a closer look.

Fiddlehead ferns—people eat those, I thought although I had no idea if this one was a fiddlehead or what they tasted like.

I picked it and unrolled it. It looked like the innermost leaf of a Romaine lettuce. I sniffed it but detected nothing recognizable—at least, nothing off-putting. I nibbled along the edge of one leaf. It was horrible. Bitter—tart—no, bitter. I spat it out and scraped my tongue with my teeth tossing the remaining shoot to the ground.

Onward I stumbled almost blindly into the fog, wondering all the while if it would ever lift.

I'm so hungry!

I pictured my mom packing pasta noodles and jars of sauce into the food box in preparation for our camping trip.

Spaghetti! Mom was gonna make spaghetti!

I tried to push thoughts of spaghetti from my mind but they wouldn't budge until suddenly I realized I'd reached the beaver dam and pond. Crossing over somewhat familiar territory, I tripped along the edge of it. I looked around for the beavers but it was all quiet now. No sign of life. I passed by the dam and continued following the river.

It must come out somewhere.

The mist rose and swirled ten feet above the surface of the water in columns. Each column was moving, alive, independent of the swirling columns of fog around it. They mesmerized me.

Why do they move like that?

Candyfloss-like vapours stretched higher and higher until the top bits evaporated and diminished momentarily only to rise into an even higher column of twirling cloud.

Suddenly a prolonged, wailing *oo-oo-oo* exploded from inside the mist on the lake somewhere quite near.

I jumped and ran behind some trees.

It's a wolf!

I gripped the fishing knife inside my hoodie pouch. Again the *oo-oo-oo* echoed across the water close at hand.

Something in the back of my mind told me that it couldn't possibly be a wolf.

How could a wolf howl from the middle of a pond?

But when the haunting *oo-oo-oo* erupted a third time, I didn't know what to think.

Then I saw a dagger-like beak cut through the vapour and glide toward me. The black duck-shaped bird let out another *oo-oo-oo*. A second loon glided behind the first.

Loons! It's only loons!

Their spine-chilling yodel reverberated over the water and I found it hard to believe that a bird could sound so much like a wolf.

When they spotted me they came to a standstill, their red unblinking eyes on me. I was startled but they more so. At that moment one dove straight down and the other back-pedalled and disappeared into the mist as smoothly as they had appeared.

I rubbed my goose-bump covered arms and kept walking. I felt weak from hunger.

I need food, I thought for the thousandth time.

Tom Thomson the artist, the outdoorsman knew how to survive in the bush, I thought. *He was probably even more capable than Dave. He could catch a fish and cook it for me. But he's dead. His body was found floating in Canoe Lake.*

I kept my eyes on the shore line and followed it as closely as I could.

This is crazy, I thought. *The fog is not lifting. Maybe I should go back.*

Then I heard a splash in the water.

What's that?

I stopped and stared. The churning vapour darkened in a spot and I could hear more splashing. The dark spot was moving toward me! I held my breath and stared wide-eyed at the spot willing the mist to burn away.

There's definitely something there!

But the undulating haze closed in again and the dark spot seemed to recede.

I'm imagining things.

Then I heard another splash and I slapped my hand over my mouth to stop myself from screaming.

This could be Park Naturalists looking for me!

I stared even more intently at the spot in the fog trying to find the courage to speak.

There's definitely something there! I thought again backing away. *It sounds like a paddle splashing in the water!*

I could see the dark shape again. The image of a canoe burned into my mind.

Maybe it's the Park Naturalists in their canoe, I hoped.

Before I could call out to them I became convinced it was Tom Thomson—only not Tom Thomson—Tom Thomson's ghost!

The mist shifted and the large dark spot appeared darker, a little more focused. I edged away from the pond. Something plunked into the shallow water very near.

It's the ghost of Tom Thomson! It's the ghost of Tom Thomson!

I was convinced he was paddling toward me in his dove grey canoe. Closer he came and closer. I took a few more steps backwards.

"Hello!" I found my voice. "Who's there?"

But there was no answer, only a loud, inhuman snort.

Chapter 8

"Who's there? Who's there?" I screamed backing away.

I couldn't decide if I should turn and run into the woods or stay within sight of the pond—my only navigational point of reference back to the cabin. I heard another plop in the water and a splash and the dark shape moved closer and rose over me.

I screamed and covered my face then uncovered it and screamed again. The shape took one step closer. It was almost on me and I looked up and could see it clearly now.

It's a moose!

Long ropes of weeds and lily plants hung from its antlers. It snorted at me and bent back its ears.

I screamed.

It shook its great weedy antlers and stomped.

It's gonna step on me!

I screamed again and the moose slowly turned away and disappeared back into the foggy pond. My heart raced. I had never seen such a large animal up close.

It almost trampled me!

I felt exhausted from screaming and nauseated.

I think I'm going to faint.

I hurried on along the edge of the pond trying to put distance between me and the moose. When I calmed down a little I decided to give myself a talking to.

"How could you think that was the ghost of Tom Thomson?" I asked myself in a whisper.

I had intended to give myself a loud scolding but it only came out as a cowardly whisper.

"That's just stupid," I told myself. "Anyway, there's no such thing as ghosts. There's no such thing as ghosts."

Soon I reached the other side of the pond and found the spot where the river fed into it. The sun was finally burning off some of the mist.

It was then that I spotted the mushrooms, a charming little pair of red-capped mushrooms. I laughed to think how like pictures of toadstools from my fairy tale books they were. I crawled over to them and delicately plucked one and examined it.

Is it poisonous?

I sniffed it.

It smells like a grocery store mushroom.

I nibbled along its edge.

It tastes exactly like a normal raw mushroom.

I waited for a whole minute but nothing happened. After that I took a big bite and swallowed quickly.

I'm fine. I feel fine. It's not poisonous.

I waited for another minute trying to monitor its effect on me. I felt nothing unusual anywhere in my body except in my stomach where the mushroom dropped to the bottom like a loonie in an empty piggybank. Finally, I popped the rest of the mushroom into my mouth and snatched up a second one.

From the moment I swallowed the second mushroom I knew regret. Regret washed over me in a dizzying wave and I was on my hands and knees.

Why did I do that?

I braced myself for the second inevitable wave. It came and many more but there was not a lot to repent of—only two small mushrooms and soon it was nothing more than a dry heave and my world was spinning.

I shouldn't have done that. Why did I do that? I've probably poisoned myself!

I lay on my back near the edge of the water for who knows how long. I watched the last bits of mist swirl and burn away. I had no sense of time just a weird feeling that I might lift off the earth and fly out into space.

I shouldn't have done that. I feel so weird.

The mushrooms had their way with me. I stared at twisting maple leaves that morphed into kites. The trees became something else. Hallucinations swirled through my mind. I was helpless to control them. My bowels cramped and I pulled my knees up to my stomach. I lay there staring up at the sky and holding on with fists full of weeds thinking that maybe gravity is a myth.

Then the ravens came. Four—no—five huge, black birds put down not far from me. They shook out their ragged feathers and then, like scheming witches, exchanged several hoarse, low-pitched croaks. I tried to get up but could not. One fixed a shiny eye on me and cocked its head to the side.

"You shouldn't have done that," the raven seemed to say.

Impossible, I thought and rubbed my eyes.

"You're hallucinating," the raven explained. "It's the mushrooms."

I groaned and looked away. I couldn't get up. I felt nailed to the spot, weak with vertigo. I tried to focus on a single thought but so many thoughts seemed to be whirling around my head like those columns of mist and I felt so sick.

I watched the ravens set to ripping apart something with their chisel-like beaks. It was some small dead thing at the edge of the pond. At that moment, I remembered the mortician who dragged Tom Thomson's body out of the grave all by himself in the middle of the night.

How could he do that?

I watched the black-robed ravens fight over their prize, tearing at its carcass, and a new wave of nausea washed over me. I rolled to one side to wretch and wondered vaguely if I should be afraid of these huge, carnivorous birds.

Go away, birds! Go away!

I forced myself to sit up and the birds hopped back with a low *keck-keck-keck*. One grabbed the scrap of carcass in its beak and lifted off and the rest followed.

Sitting with my back against a tree trunk, I cried myself in and out of consciousness.

I pray the Lord my soul to keep...

When I came to I was sweating profusely, twitching and dizzy. The sun was shining, the mist had completely burned off the pond and I could see the opposite side.

What should I do? If I keep going I might find the campground but maybe I won't. If I go back to the cabin at least I'll have shelter. What should I do?

With the sun high in the sky, shelter seemed less crucial.

I'm gonna keep going. I'll follow the river. I can always go back.

I stood on very shaky legs and stumbled forward. I hoped to see something, some sign of life such as the Park Naturalists or at least a trail marker. However, looking around I could see no indication that anyone had ever crossed that way before.

Onward I lurched, slipping on rocks at the water's edge and not caring or even noticing that one shoe was wet. Walking, walking, walking.

I want to go home.

Suddenly something in the corner of my eye moved.

What's that?

About seven metres away a mass of bushes shook.

What IS that?

I tried to clear my head, to focus, to think clearly. It all seemed so difficult.

Maybe it's that moose, I thought.

The bush trembled a second time and then a large black snout emerged.

It's a bear!

I dropped to the ground and crawled for cover.

I don't think it saw me!

I pressed myself to the ground.

What should I do? Should I make a run for it?

I knew that if it came to a foot race there could be no question of who would win. I was too weak even to see straight.

I could hear the bear thrashing about then he got quiet again.

Is he getting closer or moving farther away?

I listened and held my breath. It was impossible to tell. Then an unmistakable smell overwhelmed me.

Raspberries!

From my prone position I could see that I was surrounded by the juicy red fruit. Saliva erupted from every gland in my mouth and I snatched them from the vine and shoved them into my mouth almost forgetting the terrible situation I was in.

Finally, I forced myself to stop and to listen. I could hear the bear grunt, sniff and exhale.

How far away is he now?

I had to peek. I had to know. Ever so gingerly, I pushed myself up only to discover that my pyjama bottoms were snagged in many places by the raspberry bushes. One by one I pulled them free as fast as I could then gingerly raised myself up until I was able to see the bear grazing on raspberries.

He was a huge, bulky thing, black and shapeless. Back and forth his massive head slowly swung, sniffing, and then ripping at the little berries consuming them leaves and all. He bent over the stems with his big paws and held them while he stripped them of all fruit. To me he looked so benign, almost innocent of wanting anything more than just to eat these raspberries in peace.

Like the bear, I shoved as many berries into my mouth as I could without drawing the bear's attention to myself. I had never tasted anything more delicious in my entire life.

I tried to remember what the Park Naturalists had said about black bear during my visit to the Algonquin Park museum. However, remembering was no easy task since at the time I had been determined not to learn anything.

But there was something...yes, the Park Naturalist said that black bear are omnivores—they eat meat and vegetation. But they aren't hunters. They prefer to eat garbage and road kill.

It was a comforting thought.

Again I lifted my head to see the bear. To my dismay he was looking right back at me. We locked eyes. I didn't move. I didn't even breathe. The bear lifted his huge snout and sniffed the air. With his black coat and brown eyebrows, he reminded me of Moe my neighbour's big, gentle German shepherd.

Moe looks scary but he's just a big teddy bear, I told myself.

Then I remembered the fireflies and dragonflies and chipmunks and deer and beaver and mice and loons and moose and ravens--all harmless.

Maybe black bear are also harmless.

I looked down at the raspberries. I was so hungry. The bear also remembered the raspberries and set about eating them again. I plucked one after another and pushed them into my mouth glancing back at the bear between bites.

He just wants to eat his berries. That's all he wants. Black bear are not predators, I convinced myself.

I devoured raspberries as fast as I could but my body had been days with only a few blueberries and I had suffered through beaver fever and, recently, vomiting up hallucinogenic mushrooms. The raspberries did little to quell my dizziness or to help clear my thinking.

The bear is ignoring me, I reasoned as I moved a little closer to reach more fruit. *He doesn't mind that I'm here. He's sharing the raspberries with me. There's plenty.*

I inched a little closer and the bear looked up suddenly and snorted. I jumped. We both froze. Then the bear went back to grazing and I felt an inexplicable urge to laugh.

He doesn't mind, I told myself again. *He's inviting me to share his supper.*

A tiny wisp of doubt crossed my mind but the hallucinogenic effects of the mushrooms made me incapable of thinking it through. My hunger urged me on and I ate greedily, careless of how close I inched toward the bear.

Chapter 9

My head swam. I lost all ability to focus or think clearly. Meanwhile, the bear had his back to me. He'd gorged himself on an unexpected entrée and when he had eaten his fill he left me. From my position on the ground, I watched him retreat. He thumped off into the bush, branches snapping behind him, his heavy footstep felt even from where I lay.

I languished—I felt full yet emptied at the same time. The edges of things seemed sharper now like a photo developed in high contrast. Everything was black and white.

Where did he go? Onward to find more food.

"They spend all their time foraging for food to get enough calories to fill them up," the Park Naturalist had said. "They're possibly always feeling hungry."

Not now. He can't possibly be hungry anymore. Not after that feast, I thought picturing his red-stained maw.

When I rose and continued on my journey it struck me that the woods seemed clean for some reason--antiseptic. A drop of dew on a pine needle glistened in the sun and caught my eye. It glinted clean and pure in my new black and white world.

I felt in no hurry now. I wasn't hungry or thirsty. I felt nothing—just dizzy and not altogether there. I looked at my skinny white arms, my pale skin. I felt so light. My feet hardly touched the ground.

Am I still hallucinating?

I looked down and noticed that I had lost a shoe and, oh, so much more.

It doesn't matter.

Walking, walking, walking. There seemed no end to the trees.

Surely, I thought, *I will come to something. How far could someone possibly walk without coming out somewhere?*

Then I thought I heard someone crying. It was a sad, aching cry. I looked around but there was nothing to see. There was no one and yet the wail filled the air.

"Hello? Where are you?" I called.

At that moment, I heard a rushing, rustling, sound between the trees. Something was coming.

Is it the bear coming back for more?

It was a pack of wolves running straight toward me. The five animals wove their lean, tawny bodies in and out of the trees and bush. I screamed and ran. Spotting a climbable tree I quickly swung up one thin leg and then the other.

They're almost here!

It was impossible to get high enough to be out of reach before they got to me and I knew it. I whimpered as I struggled to get to the higher branches. Seconds later they arrived at my tree. Looking down at them, I held myself as still as death.

They will catch my scent for sure!

To my surprise they ran right past me. I hardly dared believe my eyes.

How could they not have seen, smelled or heard me?

I waited for a long time in that tree, listening and peering in their direction.

Are they gone? Are they really gone?

When I was sure they were gone, I climbed down. Glancing at my hand, I was surprised to see a huge, deep gash across the fleshy part of my palm from one side to the other. It didn't bleed and it didn't hurt either. I couldn't remember how I got that. It gave me a shock.

Mom would probably say that I need stitches, I thought.

I listened hard and looked in every direction to be sure that the wolves were really gone. Then I saw something that brought my heart right up into my throat—I was standing on a footpath.

It's a hiking trail!

I had stumbled upon one of the hiking trails that meander through Algonquin Park. Looking up I spotted a trail marker. It was nothing special--just a splash of paint on a tree trunk but I was filled with joy nonetheless.

Which way should I go?

I glanced up and down the trail. One direction looked as good as the other.

It doesn't matter. These trails are all loops anyway, I thought.

I set off straight away stumbling along the trail as fast as I could go.

How long could this trail be?

I tried to remember what I read in the Algonquin Park newspaper I'd flipped through in the backseat of Dave's car.

There are fourteen trails that all come out at highway 60. The shortest one is less than one kilometre and the longest is eleven kilometres—but the backpacking trails are a lot longer. One is eighty-eight kilometres long.

My heart dropped when I remembered that.

What if I'm on one of those long backpacking trails?

Rounding a corner in the trail I spotted a trail post cut on a slant with the number eleven on the top. Seeing it I felt buoyed up. With one shoe on and one shoe off I tripped along.

At least I'm on a trail! I'm on a trail! I'm not lost anymore!

Post number 10.

Post number ten! Only nine more to go! I'm not lost anymore!

I quickened my pace.

How long could this trail possibly be? Two kilometers? Five? Twelve?

Long shadows crossed the trail and I realized the sun was setting.

How long is this trail? The end must be near! It must be just around this next bend!

By the time I arrived at post number 9 it was so dark that I almost ran into it.

I had no choice. I had to slow down and I felt overwhelmed by discouragement.

If I don't stop soon I'll end up getting off the trail!

I kept going and after a while I stumbled on post number 8. I could go no further.

Finally I got on a trail but I didn't get to the end of it! I'm gonna have to sleep outside again!

I lay down next to the post. Facing it, I pulled out my fishing knife and carved M.E. in its base remembering to include the periods. Mary Elizabeth was here. I hoped it would help orient me when I woke up in the morning.

As the darkness closed in, I stretched out along the middle of the trail and pointed my bony finger in the direction I was going so that I would not backtrack in the morning. Then I fell asleep hearing that sad, sad cry.

If I should die before I wake, I prayed feeling senseless.

Chapter 10

In the morning I woke with a white ray of sun burning into my eyes. I felt crawly. Itchy. Tickly. Looking down I saw bugs, grubs and insects of every description crawling on my stiff body.

Bugs!

I jumped to my feet and frantically brushed them off. Just when I thought they were all gone I would find more.

"They're in my hair!"

Crying and swatting, I stumbled with one shoe on and one shoe off in the direction I was pointing. Little screeches and whimpers escaped my thin lips as I pulled at my stringy hair.

Get them off! Get them off!

A clump of hair came out in my hand.

My hair!

On the path ahead I heard a scream. I stopped dead in my tracks.

Someone's there!

But the person screamed again and I could hear her running away.

"Wait! Help me!" I cried.

What is it? Why is she running away? There must be a wolf or a bear coming!

I looked back and listened but there was nothing there.

What if it's something worse?

I couldn't imagine what could be worse. Spooked, I staggered toward the screamer.

"Wait!" I yelled. "What is it? Help me!"

The hiker screamed again and continued running.

"Wait!"

I could barely keep up. I was so weak and the trail so rugged. I ran past post number 7.

Post seven! It's post seven!

"Wait! Please help me!"

What are we running from? I wondered, glancing over my shoulder.

I stopped again and peered behind me. There was nothing there--nothing unusual whatsoever--just a deep undergrowth, low-hanging boughs, uneven trail, rocks, roots, shadows and dappled sunshine.

The hiker ran uphill and down with me hot on her heels but I was far enough away that I only ever caught glimpses of her through the trees. I could hear the hiker's heavy footfall and laboured breathing. We ran across a small creek. Up we sprinted over some wooden stairs and down a winding path on the other side. We passed the number 6 post.

Post number six! Post number six! I must be almost there!

Up around a gigantic boulder and down the other side, over a dry riverbed and along a winding trail, I flew in the shadow of the hiker.

I spotted another painted trail marker. Paint reminded me of Tom Thomson.

"...on the exact spot where Tom Thomson's body was found! So what do you think of that, M.E.?"

I remembered Dave's hopeful smile and his sad, disappointed laugh.

He was really trying to make it work but I wasn't.

Random memories swirled around inside my head.

Number 5 post. I heard a whimper and a shriek.

"Wait!"

I pictured my mom's happy smile. I remembered that when Dave came into my mom's life suddenly a sparkle returned to my mom's eyes as well.

"Come. Come with us, M.E. It won't be the same without you," I remembered my mom pleading.

Post number 4.

Number four post!

"Well it did happen almost a hundred years ago. Although they say his spirit still roams the park," Dave had said with a mischievous grin.

Maybe the hiker saw the ghost of Tom Thomson! Maybe it's real! I thought glancing back.

There's nothing there!

"Wait!" I yelled.

Post number 3.

Three!

"Wait!" I called. "I'm not the ghost of Tom Thomson!"

It's all his fault. He has people spooked!

"It's just me! It's M.E.! It's meeeeeeeee," I wailed.

The hiker screamed and seemed to run even faster.

"And all this happened right here in Algonquin Park," Dave concluded.

Dave was so happy when he told us that story. He loved entertaining us around the campfire. He'd probably been planning it all week.

I pictured his animated face looking from one to the other.

Wow, Algonquin Park is haunted—cool! I remembered thinking.

That's just stupid! I thought now. *Of course it's not haunted! There's no such thing as ghosts!*

The second last post.

Post two! Post two! Post two! Post two!

Finally, I came to the end of the trail. I passed a large map of the park displayed on a board under Plexiglas and a cubbyhole filled with trail map booklets. Stepping out from under the trees, I blinked in the direct sunlight of the parking lot. A car door slammed and spit gravel as it took off down the road.

"Wait! Wait—stop! Help me!" I yelled running after it.

Couldn't she hear me calling? What's the matter with her?

But then looking around I forgot all about it because I had finally come out at Highway 60.

Civilization! I thought.

Chapter 11

I pitched and reeled in my shredded pyjama bottoms for about a kilometre down the highway held together by a single fixed thought: *I gotta find my mom.*

No cars passed by. I came upon a road leading to a campground.

Is this the one?

The campground name wasn't familiar but then again I never knew the name of my own campground. I wasn't paying attention when Dave pulled into the park and I was too determined to hate everything about the experience to worry about it.

Down this road I disappeared not knowing whether I was in the right place or not.

I'm so close, I thought. *This has to be it!*

But there were hundreds of campsites to search and I wasn't sure what my campsite looked like. It seemed like so long ago. They had a big tent, I remembered, with a dividing wall on the inside.

Was the tent green? Blue?

I wasn't sure.

We had a picnic table with a flowery plastic tablecloth. Dave drove a navy station wagon with a red canoe strapped to the top.

It didn't make any difference anyway since that moment when colour seeped out of my world. Everything was now a shade of grey.

I lurched past two greyish tents, a white tent-trailer, a black station wagon, a greyish van, a dark pup tent, a light grey dome tent, a dark SUV, lots of grey tarp, an empty site, an RV with a pickup, two dark pup tents and a light kitchen tent—the combinations seemed endless and all looked the same.

I saw people but they didn't seem to see me. I tried to communicate with them but it was as if they were all deaf.

I gotta find my mom. If I can just find my mom everything will be okay.

I continued searching all night. Sometimes, if a tent looked familiar, I pulled the zipper down ever so quietly and poked my head inside. Sometimes I spotted a car that looked like Dave's but then I'd see fuzzy dice hanging from the rear view mirror or some such thing and I knew it wasn't his.

Mom! I want my mom!

I startled dozens of raccoons that I found standing on picnic tables and nibbling on marshmallow sticks. One was doing his best to tear apart a cooler left outside. He held it firmly between two tiny black paws.

"Store all food in your car. Keep a clean campsite."

The sentinel raccoon looked around furtively from behind its black mask but they never seemed to see me.

"Boo!" I yelled and stomped my foot but they ignored me.

The younger ones were skittish but the older raccoons had seen it all. Large and scrappy, they weren't about to become unnerved by me—that is, if they could see me at all.

I gotta find my mom.

I couldn't resist writing "M.E." on dusty car windows. It was so much easier to write my initials in dust than it was to carve them in a tree trunk. Sometimes I wrote my initials on Comfort Station mirrors.

I look terrible. I've really changed, I thought looking away unable to believe that the hollow-cheeked person with the dead eyes looking back at me was really me.

Occasionally I spotted a canoe but always it was strapped to the top of the wrong kind of car.

I gotta find my mom.

When I searched every campsite thoroughly I staggered back down the road to highway 60 toward the next campground.

I gotta find my mom.

One night a thick fog rolled in. It made seeing difficult especially without the aid of street lights along the highway. But I could see the shoulder of the road and that was enough for me. I spotted a car travelling toward me. At first the car was just two fuzzy points of light in the distance. When it approached I waved my thin arms over my head and stepped into the road.

"Stop! Help! Stop!" I yelled.

But the driver didn't see me until the last minute. When he did it was almost too late. Brakes squealed and the car veered off the road and on again. The car came to a stop and I ran towards it. Then the tires spun and it took off down the road. I watched the tail lights become tiny dots in the fog.

Crazy people! I thought. *What's wrong with these people?*

I arrived at the next campground and searched until dawn.

I gotta find my mom.

Then, in the early morning light, I spotted a canoe. Not just any canoe. This one was perched atop a dark station wagon. A large greyish tent stood next to it. There was a flowery plastic cloth on the picnic table.

Is this it? Is this it?

And then, I saw Dave slowly loading a cooler into the back of the car and my mother stepped out of the tent and tightened the straps of her backpack.

"Mom! Dave!"

Chapter 12

"Mom! Dave!" I yelled but they couldn't hear me.

My mom turned and closed the tent zipper. She and Dave appeared to be leaving. Dave was wearing his goofy mosquito net hat and my mom looked incredibly haggard and sad.

"Mom! Mom!" I screamed.

My mom and Dave walked arm in arm along the gravel road until they reached a marked trail. I ran to catch up.

"Mom! Dave!" I called after them.

My mom was crying. Dave reached back for her hand and they walked along the narrow trail like that, one in front of the other.

Then I remembered the tops of the impossibly green Jack Pines slowly swirling against an eternal blue sky. Slowly, slowly then a blur in the opposite direction as the swing unwound. I was barely holding on with one hand and gripping an ice-cream cone with the other. "I hope you're having fun, M.E.," I remembered Dave saying.

It was a happy moment but my response to Dave was a defiant silence.

Then I heard that achingly sad cry floating through the air again.

A wave of regret was followed by a sudden and even greater wave of love that broke over the levy of my heart. A love I'd never felt before.

It could have been so different.

I was closer now...to something.

I shouldn't have eaten the mushrooms. I should have stayed in the cabin. I should have borrowed my mom's flashlight. I could have loved Dave.

"Mom!" I cried. "Mom!"

I should have. I could have.

I knew. I'd known for a long time but wasn't willing to admit it to myself. I blamed it on the ghost of Tom Thomson.

It was his fault the hiker was spooked, I remembered thinking but I knew that wasn't true.

"Mommy! It's me. It's me. It's Mary Elizabeth! Mom!"

My mom and Dave slowed their steps. They were looking for something at the side of the trail.

"There," my mother said pointing.

What are they looking for?

"I'm right here," I said aloud. "Mommy, it's me!"

About five metres off the trail I could see a stone--a large, grey, oddly shaped piece of the Canadian Shield. They walked toward it still holding hands. My mom wept loudly. Her whole body shook. Dave put his arm around her.

"Hey, what's going on here?" I asked aloud but my mom and Dave could not hear me.

"Hey, what's that? What is it?" I felt panicky. "What's going on here?"

They didn't answer but walked to the other side of the rock and there I spotted it--a copper plaque stuck somehow to the side of the boulder.

"No!" I shouted. "Whatever it takes! I've changed! I'm different!"

"No!" I repeated backing away. "No, Mommy, no!"

I covered my face and wailed a long aching wail but no tears fell. Then I realized that the pitiful wail that had haunted me for so long was my own.

"It's not true!" I insisted.

But when I glanced at the four inch gash across the palm of my hand I remembered. I remembered when the colour from my world and everything else drained away. I remembered the snort, the hot blast of foul breath and the bristly black fur. I remembered the slashing, the screaming and the ripping of flesh from bone. It was the betrayal that bothered me. I thought we had an understanding. I thought he would share. But that was the mushrooms talking.

My mother bent to brush aside some leaves at the base of the rock revealing a neat little row of stones: a quartz one, a red oxide one, a striped one, and a granite-flecked one.

"No!" I shouted.

I thrust my hand into my pocket but the stones were gone.

Mary Elizabeth Rogers, born 1994, died 2008. May she rest in peace, the copper plaque read.

"May I rest in peace," I repeated and I felt lighter than ever before. The crispness of my black and white world became fuzzier. All my good resolves seemed somehow resolved.

"I'm sorry Mommy," I whispered then I faded ever more until there was nothing left except my cherished memory, hope that this was not the end, and a dusting of very good resolves.

The End.

ALSO BY BRENDA L. MURRAY

Ditching Grandpa
(Coming in 2013)

The Great Canadian
Car
Camping Cookbook

Myambi's Second
Chance*

Latitha's Story*

*All proceeds from the sale of Myambi's Second Chance and Latitha's Story will be donated to Watoto Child Care Ministries, Kampala, an organization that rescues orphaned and abandoned children in Uganda.

ABOUT THE AUTHOR

Brenda L. Murray is a writer and illustrator with a B.A. and an M.A. in English literature from the University of Waterloo. Brenda is a member of the Writers Guild of Canada. Brenda wrote the outline for The Haunting of M.E. on a few scraps of paper by the light of a lantern at her off-grid property near Algonquin Park.

CREDITS

Cover design by Indelible Creative.

Cover photo Zacarias Pereira da Mata / Shutterstock.com.

QUESTIONS FOR CLASSROOM STUDY

1. What did you enjoy about this book?

2. What have you read that is similar to this book?

3. What are some of the major themes of this book?

4. What do you think the author was trying to accomplish with this novel?

5. What is your opinion about M.E.? Do you like or dislike her? Can you identify with her?

6. How does M.E. change throughout the course of this story?

7. How does M.E.'s view of nature change during this story? Is her view accurate?

8. In what way is M.E. haunted? In what way is she haunting?

9. What are the most important relationships in the book?

10. How do you feel about the ending of the book? Were you surprised? Disappointed?

11. What is stronger in the book: plot or character development? Why? Do you think this was intentional on the part of the author?

12. Have you ever been physically lost? Do you ever feel alone?

13. Did you find this book a quick read? Why or why not?

14. There are fourteen different insects, birds and mammals that are native to Algonquin Park mentioned in this story. Did you learn anything new about these animals?

15. What did you think of the style of the writer?

18531824R00061

Made in the USA
Charleston, SC
08 April 2013